MAGIC OF THE UNICORN

MAVIS SYBIL

Formatting: Ajao Ifeoluwa

First Edition 2021

Contents

1	Poor	4
2	Berries	10
3	Home	15
4	Sunshine	22
5	Caught	27
6	Prison	34
7	Locked Up	39
8	The Prince	45
9	Thieves	50
10	Prosperity	58
11	One month later	63

1
POOR

As I walked through the woods, a cold shiver went down my spine. Winter was coming, and in the mornings, there was now frost covering the surrounding area. As I breathed in, the icy air cut through my lungs; I crossed my arms and shivered at the thought of what was soon to come.

I lived in a small village called Wolford. It was a poor village located in the middle of the woods. There was no one else around, and the closest people were from a kingdom called the Liya Empire.

The Liya Empire is a huge kingdom full of people. There has a king and queen, as well as a prince who held the throne. The Kingdom thrived from gold mines that were nearby. Many of their people were wealthy, and they owned just about everything in these woods.

My village, however, was nothing alike. It has no queens nor kings, neither do we have a prince. It was a small area full of several small shacks. The shacks were made out of timber, and they had no windows. We were too poor to afford glass. My village had little source of income because the Liya Empire owned everything around us.

Every animal, tree, bush, and even the rocks, which were a couple of feet outside our village, were all owned by the Empire. This allowed the people of my village no place to move or go. We were stuck in our little shacks for our lives.

The village consisted of about two hundred people. Most of them were my parents' age, and there were only a few others my age. This left me often lonely and adventurous. Whenever my parents were sleeping or busy doing something, I would sneak out the back door into the woods. There I would search for things such as food and even garbage from Liya that I could use to improve my household. I never found much in the woods, but sometimes I would come across something such as an old fork or spoon.

The woods surrounding the Empire were very large and went on for miles. So being in their territory wasn't much of a bother to them because they never realized I was there. The woods were too large for them to spot me, and anytime I thought I heard someone coming, I would bury myself in a pile of leaves and brush.

Life was pretty hard living in the village because we were always hungry and always lacking something that we needed. All of the hunting grounds belonged to the Liya Empire, and they didn't like to share those grounds or any other thing with us. Sometimes they would grant us an area to hunt with, but it was rare that an animal would come by. My father would go hunting once a week, and only once every few months would he return with something good enough to eat. It usually was a small squirrel that he killed with a slingshot.

Our only food source was buying from the Empire, and the cost of food was very expensive. It cost almost all of my parents' money just to be able to buy one loaf of bread. So, most of the food we ate came from when I snuck out into the woods to pick berries.

Since the Empire controls our little village, there is much hatred going on toward them. The people of my village would constantly talk about revolting against the Empire and stealing from them. Our village is so small to even succeed in any of those plans. So, those were dumb ideas. We knew that the Empire soldiers would stop us from whatever we wanted to do in an instant. Therefore, we were trapped in our little village with nowhere to go and no food to eat.

I live in a little shack on the edge of the woods with my mom, my dad, and my sister. My sister, Lydia, is 10 years old, and I'm 17. We mostly stayed home all day and studied the books that we had bought from the Empire. They sold them to us cheaply because they were old library books that no one else was reading. Lydia is smart, and she enjoys reading. Sometimes she would read about the woods and give me advice on where to go to find food and how to determine if there was a predator nearby.

Most of that information was useless, being how we were only able to go inside the small part of the woods, but other times I found it extremely useful. For example, Lydia taught me how to determine if berries were poisonous. The last thing I would want to do is bring a basket full of berries home and poison my entire family. This made it really helpful to find food because I could easily tell which berries were bad and which ones weren't.

Even though our village was small, we were able to make do with what we had most times of the year. The hardest time of year, however, was winter. That was the time of the year where disease was rampant, and food was at its shortest. There were several times where we would go days without food. Winter also came with harsh and cold weather. It snowed almost every day, and ice covered our village shacks. Staying warm was nearly impossible.

I breathed in the cold air again and shook my head at the thought of winter. I could tell that this year was going to be harsh.

2
BERRIES

I continued to walk through the woods with a large basket in my hand. Today, my only goal is to find a large berry bush before it gets too cold and starts dying. Right now was a vital time to collect food because winter was coming quickly.

I had snuck out to the woods so much that I knew the surrounding area like it was the back of my hand. I knew where all the good berry bushes were, and I knew where not to go as well.

Today has been a very unusual day of picking berries. Something about the atmosphere in the woods fell off, and I kept getting the feeling that someone or something was watching me. I kept turning my head and looking around, but no one was there. Maybe the anticipation of winter was startling me, but I could swear that I heard branches cracking on the forest floor behind me several times.

At one point, the cracking behind me had become so obvious that I whipped around and shouted, "Hello?" There was no response, so I looked around for a couple of seconds, and again, I saw nothing. I brushed off the thought that someone might be following me, and I continued to walk through the woods to the place where I knew there were the most berry bushes. This part of the woods was thick, and it was easy to hide in. That was a good thing for me because if anyone else was to come along from the Kingdom, I could quickly duck down behind some bushes and go unnoticed.

I walked in the woods about a mile away from my village before coming across a huge blackberry bush. It was the largest blackberry bush I had seen in a while, and it was odd that it was so prominent in the middle of the forest. Everything around it was starting to die, but this specific blackberry bush was huge and full of fresh ripe blackberries as if it had been in the middle of summer. I stared at it confused, but I was also very happy. There were enough blackberries on that bush to fill up six or seven baskets. That will keep my family full for a long time.

I put the blackberries in my mouth and tasted them. It was probably the sweetest berry I had ever tasted. Even in the middle of summer, the berries were never this good. Most of them were dead because the birds would get to them before I could.

Suddenly I heard a large crack in the woods. I jumped and quickly knelt down behind the blackberry bushes. I peered around for a couple of minutes in silence. I looked throughout the forest and didn't see anything other than a couple of birds and squirrels sitting on the tree branches above me.

Crack! I jumped again. This time the cracking sound was even closer to me. My heart started racing. I was deeper in the woods than normal, and if I had gotten caught by any of the people in the Kingdom, I would be in deep trouble.

Crack! Again. This time even closer. I continued to peer around the bushes again to try to see what was crackling in front of me. Still, I couldn't see anything, and it felt useless to try to spot anyone. The woods were so thick that you didn't even have to kneel down to stay hidden. It was good that the woods were thick and I could stay hidden easily, but it was also a bad thing. If I was to get caught, it would be very hard to run away, and I would most likely be captured.

CRACK! The sound was even closer than before. I started to tremble in fear as I clutched my berry basket. I sat down and put my head on my knees, hoping that I would be better hidden. I sat like that for a couple of minutes until I didn't hear a noise anymore. The cracking had stopped, and the woods were silent once again.

I lifted my head to peep around once again before I started picking. As soon as I lifted up my head, a huge white unicorn was standing in front of me, and it was looking down at me. The unicorn glowed in the sunlight that shined through the trees. Even though it was the most beautiful thing I had ever seen, I jumped in fear and screamed to the top of my lungs. The birds around me flew away from the trees as I screamed, and I used my hand to cover my mouth after realizing where I was. Obviously, if there was a unicorn around, then there were members of the Liya Empire as well.

I looked up at the unicorn in shock and saw it looking down at me once again with berries in its mouth. The unicorn was wearing a saddle that had the Empire's imprint on it.

I reached out my hand to touch the unicorn. It was the only thing I could think to do. The unicorn licked my hand and dropped some berries in it.

3
HOME

I took the unicorn by its reins and walked it closer to my village. I didn't know where it had come from and how it got into the woods. I was terrified of leaving it in the woods alone because it could have gotten hurt.

"Come on," I said to it as I pulled it closer to me. The unicorn rubbed its head on my shoulder and neighed in excitement. "You're so cute!" I said, petting its back.

The bright light that streamed through the top of the trees hit the unicorn's back and made it glow a fluorescent white color. It was so beautiful, and I could have stared at it all day. "I will call you Sunshine," I said while still petting it. Sunshine rubbed her head against my shoulder again. I guess it's a sign of happiness.

As we walked through the woods, I realized that it was starting to get very dark outside. The sun was setting, and being out in the woods at night was very dangerous. There were lots of animals such as wolves and coyotes that would come out. My parents always wanted me home before it was dark so that

I wouldn't get lost. Even though I knew the woods really well, they were very thick, and it was super easy to get lost in them when you couldn't see. Also, I didn't have a lantern or anything with me, so it was vital that I got home early.

The air outside was cold, and it made it very hard for me to walk. I didn't realize how long I have been in the woods picking berries because I was still in the middle of the woods by the time the sun was setting. I knew that I wouldn't make it home before it was dark outside, and I would have to walk in the woods in the pitch black. The thought scared me, and I shivered.

As we continued to walk through the woods, and it became dark, I started to cry out of frustration. I couldn't see where I was going, and I was stepping on all sorts of rocks and sharp sticks. Sunshine, on the other hand, was also having a hard time seeing in the dark woods, and I could tell because she was trampling over bushes as well.

We struggled to walk for a very long time, and I kept stumbling over everything. My hands and feet were getting cut up, and my legs started to ache from falling over so much.

After a couple of minutes of walking in the

dark, Sunshine stopped suddenly and sat down in the woods. I couldn't see very well, but it looked like she had her eyes closed.

"Come on!" I said, pulling on her reins. "We need to get home now!"
Sunshine still sat there with her eyes closed. I continued to try to pull her, but she was so heavy that it was pointless. I sat down next to her and pouted. "Fine," I said. "Do whatever you want-"

Just then, Sunshine's beautiful fur started to glow. I have never seen anything like it, and from all the textbooks my sister had read, I still didn't know that unicorns do this. I gasped in awe as her fur lit up the entire forest surrounding us. I could clearly see where we were going now.

Her fur glowed a beautiful golden color that made the tree and plants around us glow gold as well. It looked like the sun was beaming into the forest even though it was dark outside.

I jumped up quickly and gave her a big hug of appreciation. It was the most amazing thing I had ever seen in my entire life. At that point, I knew that Sunshine wasn't just an ordinary unicorn. She was special. She was magical.

Sunshine turned off her glowing lights as we got closer to the village. It would attract way too much attention if there was a glowing beam of light walking through it.

"Lay here," I said, pointing at a pile of leaves in the woods behind my shack. "I will come get you tomorrow."

I quickly walked inside my house, and my parents were sitting at the table waiting for me.

"Where have you been?" My dad said with an angry voice.

I showed him the giant basket of ripe blackberries I had picked in the forest that day without saying anything. His eyes lit up as I showed him this, and his entire expression changed.

"Oh," he said with a smile.

My mom looked at me with the same expression and motioned for me to put the berries on the table. This was the most food we had in quite a few days. As we feasted on our berries and bread, my dad started to speak about the Empire. He rarely did this, but when something important was going on, he would rant about it to my mom.

"Prince Charles is freaking out in the Kingdom right now. He claims that he is missing his unicorn, and it needs to be returned to him immediately. Otherwise, he will search out the entire village." My dad said, shaking his head.

My mom looked at him and frowned. "Why is this unicorn so important to him?" She asked.

My dad started chuckling under his breath as if he was about to say something crazy. "He claims that his unicorn is magical, and the longer it is away from him, the quicker it loses its magic."

My parents and sister started to burst out in laughter as though it was the funniest thing they had ever heard.

"He is going crazy!" said my mom, shaking her head.

"I know," my dad replied. "What kind of prince makes a whole scene about some unicorn. Then he claims that it is magical? Something is terribly off in his head."

For the rest of the night, my parents and sister talked about how weird it was that the prince was freaking out about his unicorn. I, on the other hand, couldn't resist the urge to run outside and find Sunshine. I had found the magical unicorn, and I needed to get it back to the Prince before it lost its magic. I knew that if I didn't get it back to the Prince, the unicorn would lose its magic, and the Prince's soldiers would come to search my village. Sure enough, they would find the unicorn or find traces of the unicorn and my entire family, and my family would be imprisoned in the castle dungeon.

"Anastasia?" My mom said, "Are you okay?"

"Yes," I replied. "I'm just thinking."

4
SUNSHINE

The next morning, I got dressed and ran outside as fast as I possibly could. I had to find Sunshine immediately, and I didn't know if she had run away in the middle of the night or if she stayed put. When I walked over to the area where I left her, there was no one there. The pile of leaves was clearly laid in, but Sunshine was nowhere to be found. I continued to look through the trees and bushes searching for her, but there was no use. She was completely gone with no trace.

What are you looking for?" A voice said behind me. I jumped. It was my little sister.

"Lydia, you scared me!" My heart was racing. "I'm just looking around for any, uh- sticks so that we have more kindling for the fireplace."

She looked at me strangely and cocked her head. "There are sticks everywhere." She said, laughing as she walked away while shaking her head.

I continued to look around for Sunshine for the next hour, but I couldn't find her. She left no trace in the woods, so I didn't even know where to start looking. After about two hours, I finally sat down in the woods and gave up.

There was no use in finding Sunshine anymore as she had probably run away to another village. If the soldiers of Liya come to search my village, they would probably know she was here. The thought of my family being put in prison made me shiver as I started to tear up.

Suddenly from the corner of my eye, I could see a faint glow of light. It kept flickering as if it was trying to catch my eye. It was a golden light that beamed through the surrounding plants. When I looked over, to my surprise, I saw Sunshine lying under some brush. I quickly ran over to her.

"Sunshine," I whispered. "Where have you been?"

I looked down at her, and to my surprise, it looked like she was in great pain. She was lying down with her head in the dirt, and her eyes were closed. She was shaking slightly, and I could tell that she wasn't doing very well. The prince said that the longer she was away from him, the more she would lose her magic; maybe it was it that was bringing her pain. I gently rub her forehead to try and make her feel better.

"I have to get you back to the prince," I whispered to her. She looked up at me with hopeful eyes. "We will leave as soon as possible. Stay here!"

I didn't know why I was feeling a sudden urge to help her, but I knew that it was my responsibility to take care of her. I stopped worrying about my parents and the Kingdom, and all my worries shifted over to her. She was in so much pain without the Prince, and it was important that she got back to her rightful owner.

I quickly ran back to my house and grabbed all of my belongings. I didn't own much, but I grabbed an extra change of clothes, hiding it in a basket that I used to get berries with. That way, it looks like I was going out for the day to pick berries.

"Where are you going?" My mom asked me.

"To pick more berries," I replied.

"Okay, but be careful. The guards are outside today looking for the unicorn."

She gave me a look of concern and bit her lip. I could tell that she wasn't happy I was going outside. However, she let me because I found so many berries last night that it was worth it to her. She would be able to feed her family.

I nodded my head and continued back into the woods to look for Sunshine. She was lying in the same spot that she was when I left. I sat down next to her and quickly thought about what I would do to get her back. I had to be very careful through the woods because if anyone saw me with her, they would think that I stole her, and they would have no idea that I was returning her. They didn't like villagers like me, so even if I told them what my intentions were, I knew that they wouldn't believe me. The easiest way to get to the Kingdom from my village was to go about ten miles north. There was another entrance to the Liya kingdom there, and I could easily sneak her back into her stable and then leave without anyone noticing.

Out of the entire situation, I didn't understand why the unicorn couldn't find the Kingdom. It wasn't very far away, so what was keeping her away?

I brushed off the thought and told sunshine my plan as if she could understand what I was saying. I grabbed her by the reins and climbed onto her back. I have never ridden a unicorn before, but I knew that the trip would be easier if I learned how to ride her rather than walk the entire journey.

"If we continue going straight, we should make it by sundown," I whispered to her as she walked toward the Liya empire.

5

Caught

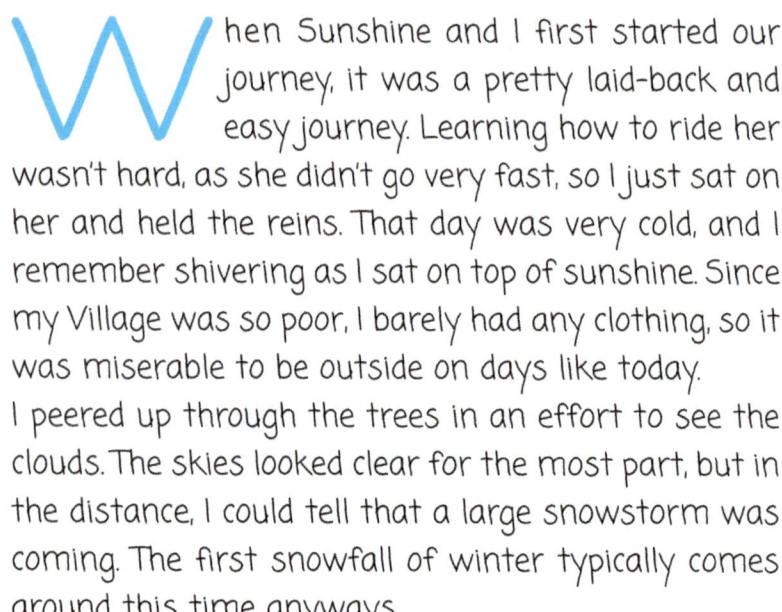

When Sunshine and I first started our journey, it was a pretty laid-back and easy journey. Learning how to ride her wasn't hard, as she didn't go very fast, so I just sat on her and held the reins. That day was very cold, and I remember shivering as I sat on top of sunshine. Since my Village was so poor, I barely had any clothing, so it was miserable to be outside on days like today.

I peered up through the trees in an effort to see the clouds. The skies looked clear for the most part, but in the distance, I could tell that a large snowstorm was coming. The first snowfall of winter typically comes around this time anyways.

It didn't seem like the cold fazed Sunshine too much, so whenever I would shiver, she would look up at me with sad eyes. That day was also not a very good day to start the journey because it became very windy. Even more so, I could tell that winter was on its way just by the weather. I would have chosen to go another day, but I was worried that Sunshine would lose her magical powers before I was able to get her back to the Prince. Besides, earlier that morning, she looked like she was in a lot of pain, so I knew that I needed to get her back before she couldn't walk anymore.

I have never heard of or seen a magical unicorn before, so I didn't know the kind of side effects she would experience after she had lost her magic. I wasn't sure if she'd just turn into a normal unicorn or if it would make her unable to move". As she was losing her magic, she became in more pain, so I kept pushing her forward faster so that we could make it to the Kingdom quicker. My goal was to make it before it got dark outside. By that way, I could sleep in the woods with her overnight and then leave by myself through the woods the next morning.

As we continued to walk through the woods, I could tell that we were getting closer and closer to the Kingdom because the underbrush beneath us started to clear out a little bit. You could clearly see the bottom of the forest floor, which is rare over by my village because it was always covered in bushes. The trees started to thin out a little bit too, and they weren't as thick. I didn't know exactly how far we were from the Kingdom, but we had been traveling for about five hours that day, so I imagined that we were three to four miles from outside of it.

As we got closer to the Kingdom, we spotted a couple of people. Sunshine was good about ducking quickly whenever someone was around. She could sense when they were around easier than I thought. We would hide behind a bush for some minutes before the people cleared, and then we would quietly gallop away again.

'However, this didn't last long because we were walking near a small stream when suddenly a large group of men stood in front of us. My heart sank as I recognized them to be a part of the Liya Empire due to their clothing.

"What do we have here?" said one of the men as he walked around Sunshine.

The men circled around her and started to laugh amongst themselves about how foolish I was.

She tried to run away, but the men quickly grabbed hold of her and stopped her from being able to move. They all looked like they were townsmen because they weren't wearing any fancy clothes. They must have been searching in the woods for the unicorn, and the prince was probably paying them to do it.

"I am here to bring the unicorn back to the Prince," I said to the men hoping that they wouldn't think I was stealing her.

One of the men with a large red beard laughed and kicked me off of Sunshine's back. My face hit the floor, and I let out a shout of pain. The men laughed around me as I tried to get up and brush the dirt off of me.

One of the men grabbed Sunshine by her reins and ripped her over closer to him. "We aren't going to take the unicorn back to the Prince," he said while mocking me. "Are you aware of how much you can sell her for? You would be able to buy your entire village brand new houses." He smirked over at me.

The men and him started laughing amongst themselves again. This time, they were mocking me for being a part of the village.

I looked at him, disgusted that he had betrayed his own Prince. I, on the other hand, did not like the Liya Empire and the Prince, but Sunshine needed help.

"Give her back!" I shouted at him, hoping that he would listen. I knew that it was no use, though.

As the men continued to mock me, they also started to be very mean to Sunshine. They were kicking her, pulling her hair, and trying to force her to use her magic. Every time she wouldn't use her magic, they would hurt her even more, and I could hear her neighing in pain. My eyes filled with tears as I witnessed the horrible men torturing her. Sunshine looked at me sadly, but I could also see anger in her eyes.

I kept shouting at the men to stop hurting her, and I kept trying to run over and help her. But it was no use because the men would hold me back away from her.

Suddenly, Sunshine's horn began to glow very brightly. The men backed away in fear of what was happening. Sunshine stood up, and she used her horn to flash bright pink-colored beams of light toward one of the men. The beam hit the man in the chest, and he slowly began to shrink. The man shrank so low to the floor that he looked like the size of an ant. The rest of the men began to run away, but it was too late because Sunshine had already gotten them with her horn. One by one, the men slowly shrink into the forest floor, and after that, they were nowhere to be seen.

I ran over to Sunshine in shock and gave her a big hug. I knew that she had gone through a lot in the past few minutes, and I was grateful that she had used her magic to save us.

We both took a few minutes to breathe and relax before I hopped back on her, and we continued through the forest to find the prince.

6

PRISON

The rest of our journey to the Empire was mostly peaceful. Just like before, it was very cold, and we would have to duck down under the bushes sometimes so that we wouldn't be seen by people in the surrounding area.

Once the sun went down, Sunshine and I found a tree, and we chose to sleep under it. We had to wait until the middle of the night to enter the Kingdom. Otherwise, we would risk being seen by someone who was up late at night.

We laid beneath the tree, and I was both cold and hungry. Sunshine was getting sicker, and I was glad that I was going to get her back to the Prince by tomorrow. She was barely able to keep her eyes open, and I was worried that we wouldn't be able to make it if we waited too long.

Both of our stomachs rumbled simultaneously, and I let out a chuckle. I hadn't eaten anything all day, and neither had Sunshine. Sunshine sat up a bit and pointed her horn at the brush behind me. She closed her eyes, and her horn started to glow a little. It wasn't much of a glow, and it wasn't as much as last time, but it was enough to still be beautiful.

Her horn glowed the same beautiful shade of

gold it always did. No matter how bright it glowed, it was always marvelous to me. I couldn't take my eyes off of it.

She squinted her eyes shut as hard as she could and started to shake a little. She was struggling to get any magic out. I felt bad for her, and I was about to tell her to stop so that she wouldn't hurt herself when all of a sudden, a small blackberry bush appeared where she pointed her horn. The blackberries were full and ripe, and there were hundreds of them.

"You were the one who put the berries in the woods!" I said in a whisper. It was her all along. She nodded her head and rubbed it against my shoulder.

I stared at the bush in awe as I started to pluck the sweet berries off the branches. They tasted amazing, and they were perfectly ripe.

That night, Sunshine and I laid down and ate a bunch of blackberries. I never felt so full in my entire life, and it felt nice to finally have food in my stomach. Sunshine and I watched the stars that night. Now that the forest wasn't as dense, I could see the stars better than I ever had been able to. It was a beautiful sight, to say the least. Shortly after we had finished feasting on our blackberries, I laid my head down on Sunshine's back and fell asleep.

I was startled awake by the sound of chains close to my ears. Before my eyes could adjust to the darkness, I heard the sound of Sunshine neighing. I sat up as quickly as possible and saw the same men that Sunshine had shrank in front of me. This time there were more of them. The men all looked very similar, and they were not happy to see me with Sunshine.

I felt my hands being taken from the ground, and cold chains were wrapped around my wrist. They were pulled so tightly that it caused me to wince.

"This is the girl that stole the Unicorn," one of the men that Sunshine had shrunk said. He looked at me and gave me an evil smirk.

"No, I was returning her to the prince!" I yelled back.

"Oh, hush up," said the man with a red beard. "We saw her in the woods earlier, and she told us that she was going to sell the Unicorn so that the people in her village could afford to live in new houses."

The guards looked down at me and glared.

I was so angry that I could feel my face turning red. How could they have accused me of this? I was also angry that Sunshine's magic wore off on the men. I was hoping that they would stay tiny forever.

"Take her away to the palace dungeon," said the main guard. "The prince will decide what to do with her."

Suddenly I was lifted up, and the guards started walking me toward the palace. They held me by their arms and dragged my feet along. I turned around to see Sunshine neighing and fighting her way away from the guards. She squinted in an effort to use her magic, but there was nothing left. There was no use.

As we walked through the Kingdom to the palace, many people witnessed what was happening, and they stood around in shock. They all knew what was going to happen to me for "stealing the unicorn." I was being taken to the palace dungeon, and there was no way I was going to be able to get out of it.

7

LOCKED UP

The dungeon was a cold and lonely place. There were several cells with prisoners lined up on the walls and a large spiral staircase that took me down through it. It was cold and wet in there, and rats ran across the floor in an effort to get food. As I walked past the prison doors with my chains on my wrist, I could hear the prisoners yelling for me to save them.

"Get me out of here!" They would yell as they reached their dirty fingers through the bars.

As the prisoners called for me to save them, I trembled, thinking about how that was definitely going to be me one day.

It smelt of mildew in prison, and it was the most disgusting place I had ever been in. When they brought me into my cell at the end of the dungeon, there were bugs, mold, and rats within my cell. I shivered at the thought of having to live here for a long time.

My parents had no idea where I was because I told my mom that I was going out to pick some berries. They obviously knew I was missing by now because I was supposed to be back at my house hours ago. But, no one knew I was here, so no one could come and save me.

"You will stay here until the prince needs to speak to you," one of the guards who was hunched over said. He looked about seventy years old, and we were missing most of his teeth.

I glared at him as he walked me into my cell and closed the door behind me. It made a large rattling sound as it closed, and dust flew everywhere.

My cell had the most mold and bugs out of the other cells in prison. I walked over to the corner of the cell and sat down there. It was the only dry place that wasn't filled with an inch of water. Next to me, I heard prisoners yelling and screaming and begging for the guards to let them go. It was a miserable place to be in, and I started crying. I cried for about ten minutes before I heard a voice next to me, through a large crack in the wall.

"Pssst," It said.

I looked around and eventually realized that it was coming from the crack in the wall.

"Hey," the voice said. "Come over here."

I scooted closer to the wall and peeked through the crack. In the cell next to me was an older woman who would be just as old as the guard who put me in my cell. She had white hair, a long thick nose, and big blue eyes. She looked tired and had purple bags under her eyes as if she hadn't slept in the past year.

"What is it?" I whispered as I scooted closer.

"You're the girl who's locked up in here for stealing the unicorn, aren't you?" She said with wide eyes.

I gave her a concerned look because I was annoyed that the prisoners also thought I stole the unicorn.

"I didn't steal it," I said, shaking my head. "I was returning it to the prince because it was sick."

The lady looked at me and nodded her head. "As they walked down here to give us our meals for the day, I overheard them talking about you. They claim you came from a small village about 10 miles south, and they are concerned that you are attempting to use the unicorn to make money for the village". They think that your village is trying to steal from the King, and they're thinking about attacking your village."

I looked up at her in horror as she said that. "They want to attack my village?" I asked.

She nodded her head as I stared in disbelief.

"The prince is going to want to talk to you," she

said. "You need to explain to him that you are inno-cent, and you have to do whatever you can to convince him that you are. If you don't, you will be down here for the rest of your life, and your village will cease to exist. You need to be careful. Your family and friends could be killed." She stared at me in horror. We both knew what was going to happen if the prince didn't believe me.

This whole time, I was just trying to help the unicorn get back to her home so that she wouldn't lose her magic. But now, the Liya Empire believes I intend to use the unicorn to help my village. My village doesn't gain anything from me helping the unicorn.

I slumped down in the corner of the prison cell again and put my hands over my face. I stop crying' at the false accusations against me. I couldn't help but think that my family would be harmed and that I would be the one to blame for the destruction of my village'. I didn't want to spend the rest of my life in prison, just like the other prisoners. This was a mis-erable place, and I wanted out.

I spent about three hours in the palace prison that day, pacing back and forth and constantly worrying about what was going to happen to me and my village. After a little while of thinking, I heard the large metal door to the prison open, and I heard several sets of footsteps walking toward my cell.

"The prince would like to speak to you now." One of the guards said to me as he opened up my cell and put the chains back on my wrist. "And I must warn you, he isn't happy."

8

THE PRINCE

The guards walked me out of prison and into the main entrance of the palace. The palace was a large building made of a beautiful stone pattern. It appeared to be at least five stories high, and it sat on top of a small hill overlooking the surrounding town. Inside the palace, there was a large room that had a beautiful marble floor. I had never seen a building so large and so beautiful in my entire life.

I didn't take the time to enjoy the palace's beauty because I was being brought before the Prince. My stomach sank when I saw him because he did look very angry. He was glaring at me with wide blue eyes, and he was sitting on his throne with his arms crossed. The Prince had dark brown hair and blue eyes, and he was fairly tall. He wore a blue suit with gold shoulder pads. His shoes were perfectly shined, and his hair was neat.

"Your majesty," the main guard said while bowing. "I have brought before you the prisoner that stole your unicorn."

The prince motioned for them to leave the room, and I was left standing there still with chains wrapped around my hands.

"Walk closer to me," the prince said in a stern tone.

As I walked closer to the prince, I could see clearly how attractive he was. His skin was fair, and he had caring eyes even though he was upset with me.

"Before I make any decisions about your punishment, I will give you five minutes to explain yourself," he said.

I nodded my head in understanding before I started to speak. "I was in the woods in my village picking berries so that my family could have dinner when I saw your unicorn. It looked lost, so I brought it back to my village with me. No one saw that I brought her back with me because I hid her.

Later that night, I heard my father talking about the Prince losing his magical unicorn." I started to cry from frustration as I saw the prince give me an annoyed look. It didn't look like he was interested in my explanation. "I noticed that Sunshine... I mean, your unicorn was starting to get sick, so I went with her here to give her back to you. Along the way, while we were sleeping, some men thought I was trying to steal her. I tried to explain to them that I wasn't going to steal her, but they didn't believe me."

The prince stared at me in confusion. My story was not false, but it was one that could be easily mistaken. It would have been easy to assume that I was trying to steal Sunshine away from the Kingdom.

"Your story doesn't add up," he said to me with an angry tone. "If you were really trying to return my precious unicorn to me, then why did you and the unicorn shrink my men? Why did you tell my men you were going to sell her for money?"

"No, you don't understand." I started. "The whole reason your unicorn used her powers against the men was that they were trying to kidnap her from me so that I couldn't get her back to you. They wanted to sell her and keep the money for themselves."

"How do I know who to believe in the situation?" he asked me.

He still had an annoyed look on his face. His arms were crossed, and I could tell that he didn't believe anything I was saying. I started to feel hopeless, and then a great idea popped into my head.

"Believe your unicorn," I said suddenly. I had an idea of how I could convince him to believe me. "According to your men, if the whole time I was really just trying to steal her... then wouldn't she have used her powers against me? Why did she feel the need to shrink them and not me?"

He looked at me confused and cocked his head. "Sunshine had to shrink the men first because they tried to take her away to another village to sell her. The men were angry that Sunshine shrank them, so they are trying to frame me and make it look like I stole her."

As I said that, he raised his eyebrows and nodded his head. I could tell that what I had told him convinced him partially that I was innocent. Of course, I couldn't tell whether or not he believed me fully, but at least he was considering my story.

Just then, a group of guards ran into the palace and started yelling. "Prince Charles! Your unicorn is missing again! Someone has stolen her from her stable!"

9

Thieves

Within an instant, the Prince unlocked my chains from my hands and took me outside.

"Get a horse prepared for us!" He shouted at one of the guards.

We ran all the way down the hill to where Sunshine was supposed to be. The prince stared at the broken stable in a fury.

He turned to me and said, "You remember what the men look like, right?" I nodded my head. "Okay good, we are going to go find them."

The prince lifted me onto the back of the horse, and then he got on after. He took the horse by the reins, and the horse started running. I almost went flying off of the horse because I still didn't know how to ride one even after being with Sunshine for a day.

The horse was a beautiful black stallion, and it had a gold-plated saddle on its back that read, "Charles."

"Hold on!" He yelled back at me as the horse started galloping into the woods.

We continued to gallop in the woods toward my village for about twenty minutes. As we got deeper into the woods, the branches of the trees started to hit me in the face and arms, and I couldn't see. I winced in pain as we passed through the deep forest. The horse was galloping so fast that I would fall off if I moved an inch.

After what seemed like eternity, we finally came to a halt. Laying in the brush below us was Sunshine's saddle. The prince looked down at it and shook his head. I could tell he was angry, and he wanted nothing more but to find her.

"Where do you think we should go?" I asked him.

"I'm guessing they headed west to the next village. There is a large horse market there, and I'm sure that's where they want to sell her." He shook his head once again. "They took off her saddle so the village wouldn't suspect that she was a stolen horse."

I nodded in agreement. It made sense that the men would do that.

Just then, we heard crunching in the leaves behind us, and we both turned around to see an entire group of men standing behind us. They were holding Sunshine by a rope around her neck. It was the same men who claimed that they were going to save her.

They all stood there surrounding Sunshine as if they were ready to fight for her at any moment.

At this point, we were about five miles from my village, and I recognized the surrounding area perfectly.

"Give me her now!" the prince shouted sternly.

The men looked at him and started laughing. "You really think it's that easy?" asked one of the men.

The prince and I glared at him as he held a knife up to Sunshine's horn. "Make any sudden moves, and your precious unicorn will be gone."

If Sunshine's horn was injured, then she would lose all of her magic, and she would be severely injured. Sunshine's life would be put at risk if we made any sudden movements, but if we walked away, the prince would be left without Sunshine, and she would be sold to someone who would not treat her well. She would lose all of her life being away from the prince, and things would not be good for any of us after that.

I heard the prince take a deep breath near me as he was trying to figure out what to do. I had no ideas, and I'm sure he didn't either.

"Your only option is to get back on your horse and go back to the kingdom," said the man in the red beard with a large smirk on his face.

"You know I can't do that," the prince said.

Suddenly I felt cold hands around my mouth, and I was ripped off the black horse.

"Then she will come with us!" hissed the man that grabbed me.

The Prince became more uneasy than ever before. I could see the anger building up in his eyes, and he stood there not knowing what to do. He was helpless. He had no guards with him, and he had no weapons either. We had rushed on the horse so quickly to find Sunshine that we didn't even think about bringing anything useful with us.

The men standing around us were clearly prepared to fight for Sunshine. They were all very poor and didn't have any weapons, but one of the men had two swords on his side. That was more than we had, and so we knew that we stood no chance.

Right when the men were going to take me away with Sunshine, a bunch of men came out from the surrounding trees. The trees were so thick that we didn't see them standing there the whole time.

I gasped when I realized who the men were. They were all members of my village who came to help. We were all too poor for weapons, but out of cloth and sticks, they all made slingshots with rocks.

My father would use the slingshot to go hunting for squirrels, so I knew that they could be very effective. This gave me a little bit of hope.

At this point, there were forty men to six. The thieves froze and looked at them with fear in their eyes. They knew that they had been greatly outnumbered.

"Put the girl down!" yelled my dad from a distance. He had an angry look on his face, as I had never seen before. The man dropped me, and I fell on my knees to the floor. I quickly got up and ran behind the horse to be protected from the men around me.

"If you know what's good for you, you will give back the Unicorn," my dad said again.

The men all looked around as a cold breeze swept through the woods. It was starting to snow. The clouds above us were a dark purple, and we all knew it was not going to be a light snowfall. I shivered at the thought of being trapped out in the snow.

The men started laughing at each other again. "You think we are going to give her up that easily?" They said as they continued to laugh.

At that moment, my dad and all the village members started running toward the men with their slingshots. None of the men were forced to run away from the slingshots. The slingshots did little damage and only slightly injured the men. They still held onto Sunshine, even as the fighting began.

The main man with a red beard pulled out a long sword and pointed it at my father and the prince. I looked over at Sunshine, and I saw that she was squinting her eyes closed. She was trying to use her magic, but there was no use.

My father knocked the sword out of the man's hand with a slingshot, and the prince picked it up. It didn't do much good because the man pulled out the second one from his side.

The prince and the man started fighting with the swords. The fight was brutal, and everyone watched in horror as the two men fought. As the prince and the bandit fought, the other men started to fight each other as well. They didn't have weapons, so they just wrestled each other on the floor in an effort to keep them at bay. I stood around in horror, looking for some way to help. The fighting went on ruthlessly for what seemed like eternity until the prince was cut on the arm. He dropped his sword and grabbed hold of his cut, wincing.

"This is the last time." The man said, pointing his sword at the prince's chest. I watched in fear as the man was about to kill the Prince when all of a sudden, a giant beam of light hit him straight in the back. The beam was a bright purple color, and it glowed in the forest around us. Sunshine had gotten free from the men's grip while they were fighting each other and was able to muster up enough power to defend herself and the prince.

The men looked at her in shock as they saw what she had done to the man holding the sword up to the Prince. He melted to the forest floor like a witch who drank hot water. They began to run away in the opposite direction of the Kingdom as fast as possible, leaving Sunshine behind.

10

Prosperity

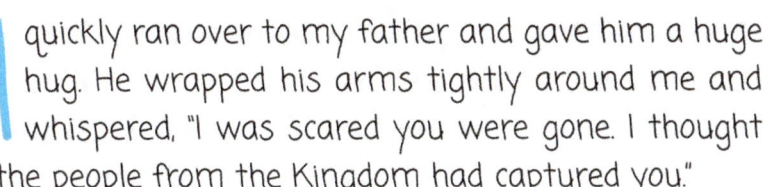

quickly ran over to my father and gave him a huge hug. He wrapped his arms tightly around me and whispered, "I was scared you were gone. I thought the people from the Kingdom had captured you."

"They did," I whispered back. "I can explain everything later."

I turned around to see the Prince sitting on the floor with Sunshine beneath him. I walked over to him and saw that Sunshine was not waking up. The prince looked up at me and frowned. "This is exactly what I was afraid of," he said, shaking his head.

Everyone gathered around him and Sunshine to see what was going on. "She used too much of her magic, and now she won't wake up," he said. He put his forehead on her neck and breathed out a breath of sadness. We continued to stand around in silence because we didn't know what to do. It appeared as though there was no way to help Sunshine anymore, and tears started falling from my eyes as I saw the prince in agony.

"What do we do?" I asked the prince, hoping I could help in some way.

"There is only one thing we can do. We have to give her magic back to her."

I gave him a confused look. Give her magic back to her? What was that supposed to mean? None of us had magic to give her.

"The only way to restore her magic is to feed her something she used her magic on." I haven't seen her use her magic in that way for years. I don't know where I could find anything..."

My eyes lit up as he said this, knowing that I had some berries in my pocket that came from her magic.

"Wait!" I shouted eagerly. "She used her magic to grow a blackberry bush when we were hungry. I saved some of the berries in my pocket for later!"

The Prince jumped up in excitement as I said this. I handed him the berries, and he started to mash them in his hands. He quickly opened up Sunshine's mouth and set the mashed berries on her tongue.

"Come on, come on..." He said as we waited for her to wake up.

After a couple of minutes, I saw Sunshine's hooves twitch, and I saw her eyelids start to flutter open.

"She's awake!" I cried in joy as she opened her eyes.

The Prince bent down to hug her, and we all celebrated around her. I was so thankful that I had saved some of the berries from the bushes she grew.

Sunshine would be okay, and the prince finally had his unicorn safe and sound.

I turned toward my dad to hug him. As we started walking back to the Empire, we talked about the hours that had passed.

"How did you know where I was?" I asked him.

"Your sister Lydia is smarter than she looks," he laughed. "She said that she saw your eyes light up at the dinner table when we talked about the Unicorn. The next day you left and never came back. We didn't know where else you were, so our only option was to try and look for you in the woods."

I looked up at him and smiled. I'm glad that he found me because without him, who knows what would have happened. Sunshine would have been captured, and the Prince would have been left without her or possibly killed. I shivered at the thought of that happening.

"Thank you," I said as we started walking back toward the castle.

"You're welcome," he said with a smile.

"While you guys are saying your thank yous, I thought I should say mine too," said the prince. "Thank you for everything that you guys did. I'm sorry that I locked you in my dungeon," the prince said, chuckling. "Can I get your name?" he asked.

"Anastasia," I said as we put Sunshine back in the palace stables to rest.

11

One month later

Months have passed since the incident with Sunshine. The incident that went on with Sunshine helped our village more than anything else. After my dad and I saved Sunshine, the Prince, King, and Queen decided that our village was not full of a bunch of poor helpless people. Instead, they learned to believe that our village is full of poor but amazing people who have kind hearts.

Over the past month, the village and the Liya Empire made agreements to better the lives of the village people. We decided that it would be fair to share the forest between us, as well as the food that grew in the forest. The hunting grounds were opened up to anyone who wanted to use them. The Kingdom stopped charging the people in my village for food so highly to enable people to feed their families. They were also given the option to move into the Empire, but many people chose to stay.

Now that we had food and didn't have to worry about starvation, the village was a wonderful place to live. People from the Empire and the village connected with each other, and our community grew very large. Almost every week, the prince would come with Sunshine to the village, and we would play in the snow together. Most times, Sunshine would use her magic to do all sorts of things. She would build giant snow-men, and one time she even made me a beautiful dress that matched the color of the ice. I felt like Cinderella in the sense that she was my godmother.

The Prince and I would dance around in the snow as Sunshine lit the forest up with her glowing fur.

"You look very beautiful in that dress." The prince would say to me whenever I was wearing it.

"Thank you, your majesty." I would say as we walked deeper into the snowy woods with Sunshine right by our sides.

We were always ready for another adventure.

www.ingramcontent.com/pod-product-compliance
Lightning Source LLC
Chambersburg PA
CBHW071316200626
46813CB00015B/2233